Truly Foul & Cheesy™ Geography Facts & Jokes

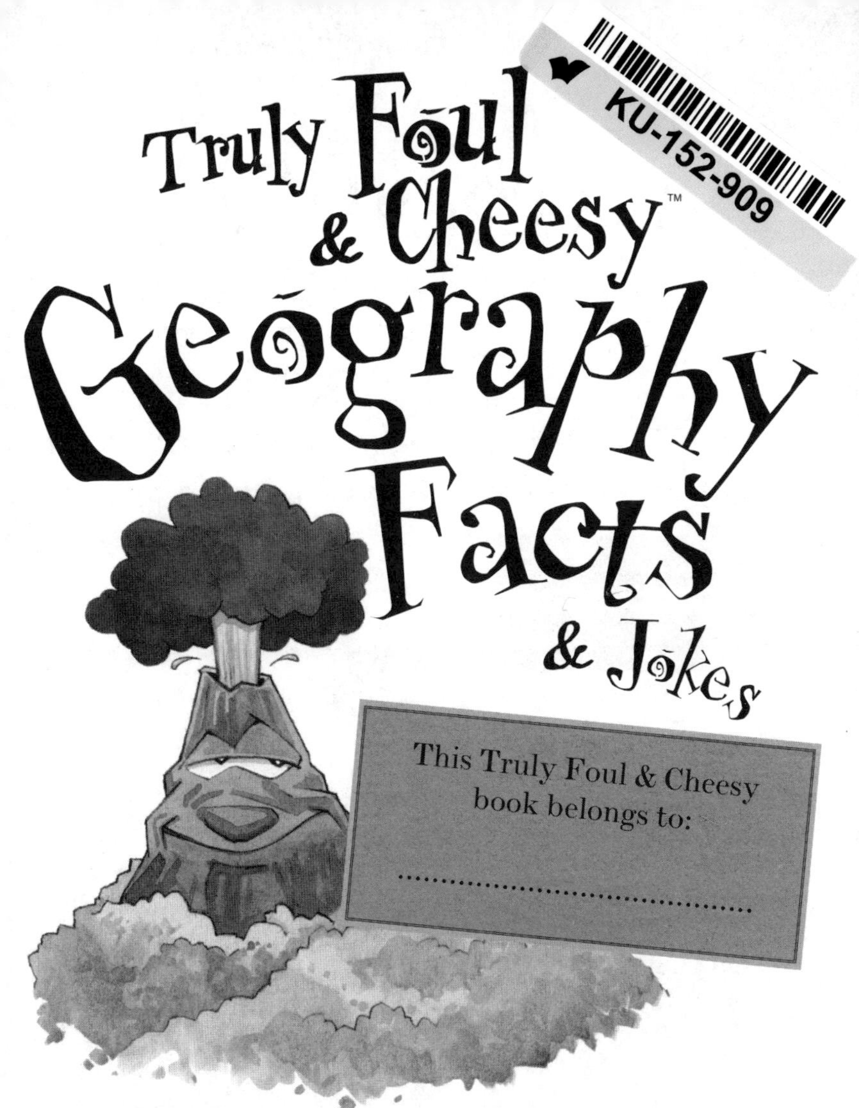

Written by
John Townsend

Illustrated by
David Antram

BOOK HOUSE
a SALARIYA imprint

Introduction

Unfortunately my better map of the Bermuda Triangle has mysteriously disappeared.

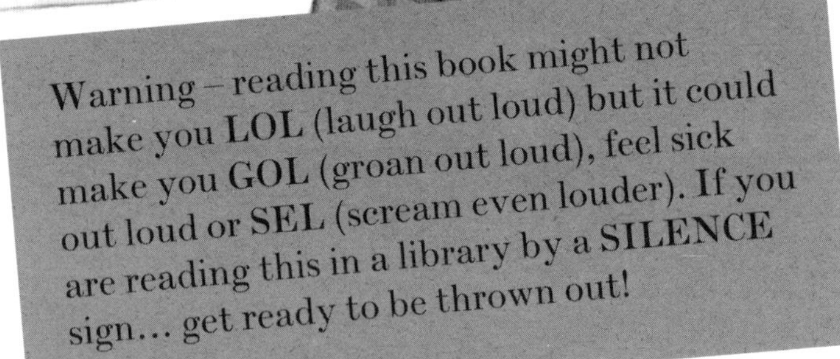

Warning – reading this book might not make you LOL (laugh out loud) but it could make you GOL (groan out loud), feel sick out loud or SEL (scream even louder). If you are reading this in a library by a SILENCE sign… get ready to be thrown out!

Disclaimer: The author really hasn't made anything up in this book (apart from some daft limericks and jokes).

He checked out the foul facts as best he could and even double-checked the fouler bits to make sure – so please don't get too upset if you find out something different or meet a geography teacher in a cagoule with a clipboard up a mountain (like the author used to be).

Official warning

This book is a jumble of fascinating geographical bits and bobs, with a few gross and toe-curling facts thrown in. As GEO means 'earth', geography is all about our amazing planet, its people and places. It's a great subject that tries to find out what goes on where and why. So hold on to your hat (waterproof) and cagoule as we put on our hiking boots, whizz around the world, gallop the globe and pop into places that might astound and amaze you…or just blow your socks off. Oh yes, and look out for the yuckily smelly bits. You have been warned!

Geo limerick

Yes, geography's all about places,
From quadrats* to vast open spaces...
So, if you can map it,
Download it or app it,
You've a subject the whole world embraces.

*Small area of habitat, (e.g. one square metre) used as a sample for surveying the local distribution of plants or animals.

Riddles

First up – time to get 6 cheesy riddles out of the way...

Q: What do maps, bathrooms and fish have in common?
A: They should all have scales.

Q: How did the geography student drown?
A: Her grades were well below C-level.

Q: What sits in the corner but can move all round the world?
A: A stamp.

Q: What is round at each end and high in the middle?
A: Ohio (Midwestern state in the Great Lakes region of the United States).

Q: What is a pirate's favourite country?
A: AAARRRgentina.

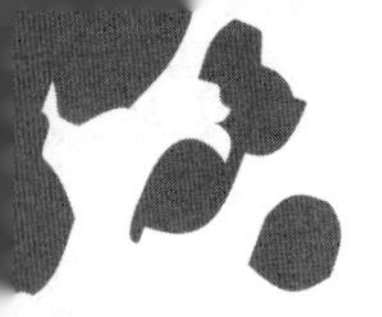

Q: What did one volcano say to the other?

A: As soon as you blew your top it was lava first sight.

Earth mega facts to ponder in the bath

1 Earth is often called the ocean planet. Its surface is 70% water but only 3% is fresh and drinkable. The rest is salt water.

The Earth has a molten inner core made of iron and other metals. There is enough gold in the Earth's core to cover the entire surface of the Earth in half a metre of the valuable mineral everyone loves. It might be tricky to get hold of as the Earth's inner core is about the same temperature as the Sun. Ouch!

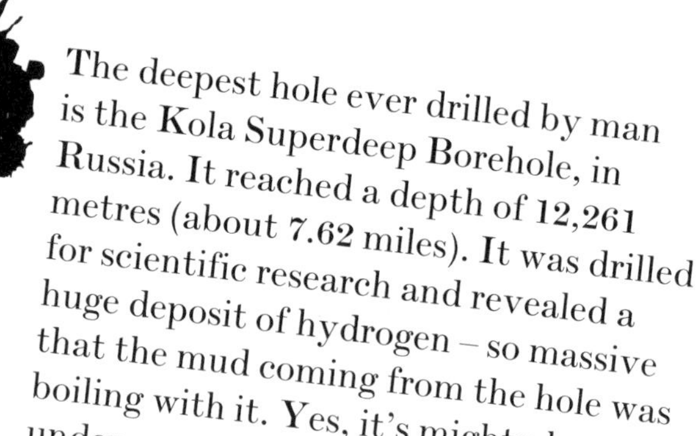

The deepest hole ever drilled by man is the Kola Superdeep Borehole, in Russia. It reached a depth of 12,261 metres (about 7.62 miles). It was drilled for scientific research and revealed a huge deposit of hydrogen – so massive that the mud coming from the hole was boiling with it. Yes, it's mighty hot deep under your feet.

Every day, Earth is bombarded with more than 100 tons of dust and sand-sized particles. About once a year, an asteroid the size of a car hits Earth's atmosphere, creates an impressive fireball, and burns up before reaching the surface. Every 2,000 years or so, a meteoroid the size of a football field hits Earth and causes big damage. The Earth's atmosphere protects the planet from most meteors. They usually burn up before they reach the Earth's surface. Oh yes, and look out... lightning strikes the earth over 8.6 million times per day – luckily not always in the same place.

5 Earth is protected by a strong magnetic field that keeps our atmosphere securely in place. The Earth's diameter (the distance round its middle at the equator), is 12,760 kilometres (7,928 miles). In fact, the Earth is not an exact sphere but slightly oval.

Geography teacher: What is at the centre of Earth?
Pupil: The letter 'r'.
Geography teacher: Doh!

Geo facts to boggle your mind

The longest known cave system on Earth is the Mammoth Cave in Kentucky. It stretches for more than 628 kilometres (390 miles), and that's just what has been explored so far. Scientists believe it may be over 966 km (600 miles) long. Keep away if you're scared of the dark.

The highest temperature ever recorded on the planet was in Furnace Creek, Death Valley, California, U.S.A. – a sizzling 56.7 degrees Celsius (134°F) on 10 July 1913.

Tourists often try frying eggs on scorching rock in the high temperatures in Death Valley. It doesn't always work – just on fry-days!

NASA satellite data from Antarctica shows Earth set a new record for the coldest temperature ever recorded: -94.7°C (-135.8°F). It happened in August 2010. On a high ridge in Antarctica on the East Antarctic Plateau, temperatures in hollows can dip below -92 °C (133.6 °F) on clear winter nights. Now that's mega-chilly!
The coldest permanently inhabited place is the Siberian village of Oymyakon in Russia, where the temperature reached -68°C (-90°F) in 1933, the coldest ever recorded outside Antarctica. And yes, apparently if you have to pee in such places, urine would freeze shortly after hitting the ground – brrrr!

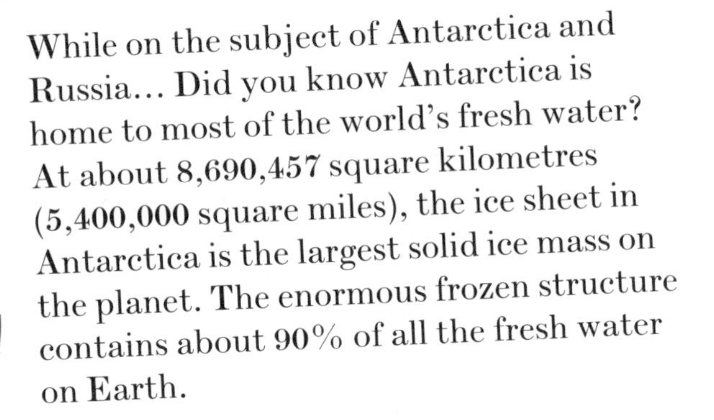

While on the subject of Antarctica and Russia... Did you know Antarctica is home to most of the world's fresh water? At about 8,690,457 square kilometres (5,400,000 square miles), the ice sheet in Antarctica is the largest solid ice mass on the planet. The enormous frozen structure contains about 90% of all the fresh water on Earth.

Lake Baikal in Russia holds 20% of Earth's unfrozen fresh water. It is the deepest and oldest lake in the world. And yes, you've guessed... mysteries and monsters are said to lurk within.

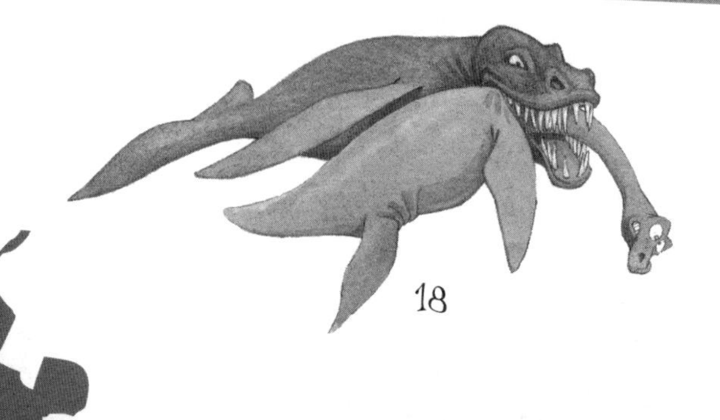

At 8,848 metres (29,028 feet) above sea level, Mount Everest is the highest mountain on Earth, right?(In 1999, it was found to be a couple of metres taller than geographers first thought!) In fact, Mount Kea in Hawaii is almost a mile taller than Everest if measured from its undersea base. But the peak of another mountain is technically closer to the Moon.

Mount Everest is the tallest mountain on Earth, so surely its top would be the highest point on Earth (and closest to the moon)? But when you remember that Earth is slightly oval-shaped, things get interesting. Our planet is fatter around the equator, meaning countries like Ecuador in South America have a bit of an edge. With this added elevation, the top of Ecuador's Mount Chimborazo, which is only 6,268 metres (20,564 feet) tall, is surprisingly the closest to the Moon. Not many people know that!

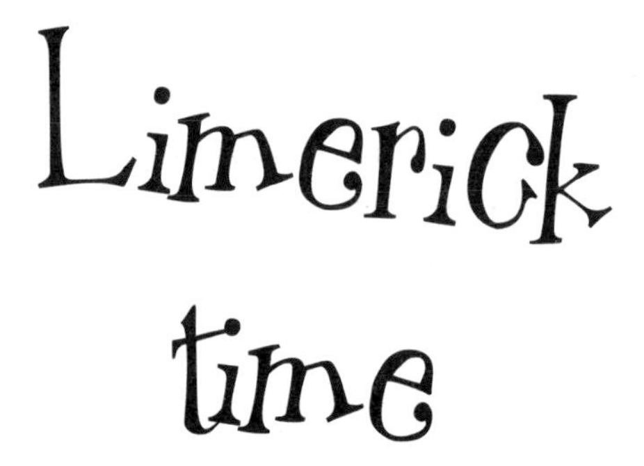

A geography teacher, aged forty,
Was very out-doorsy and sporty.
He hiked over ice
In his underpants – twice...
Did you think the last line would be naughty?

A geography field trip from school
Went onto the pier at Blackpool
To study things coastal
But the teacher got boastful
And dived in the sea – what a fool
(the tide was out!).

Five silly riddles

Q: What do you call a map guide round a high security prison?
A: A con-tour map.

Q: If Mississippi bought Virginia a New Jersey, what would Delaware?
A: Idaho… Alaska! (I dunno, I'll ask 'er.)

Q: What do you call the little rivers that flow into the Nile?
A: Juveniles.

Q: Why is it hard to sleep next to someone from the South Pacific?
A: They're so **Fiji-ty.**

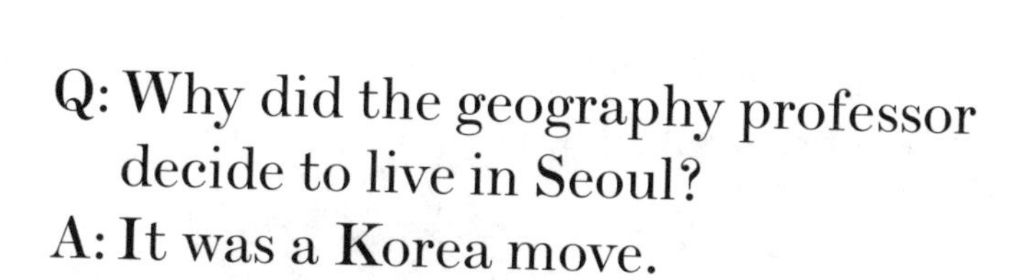

Q: Why did the geography professor decide to live in Seoul?
A: It was a Korea move.

Geography teacher: I just climbed to the top of the world's highest mountain.

Student: Everest?

Geography teacher: Yeah, about every 100 metres.

Student: Doh!

What's in a name?

Geography is all about places – and some places have weird and wacky names.
Try some of these to boggle your brain:

The shortest place name is simply 'Å' and there are two of them – in Sweden and Norway.

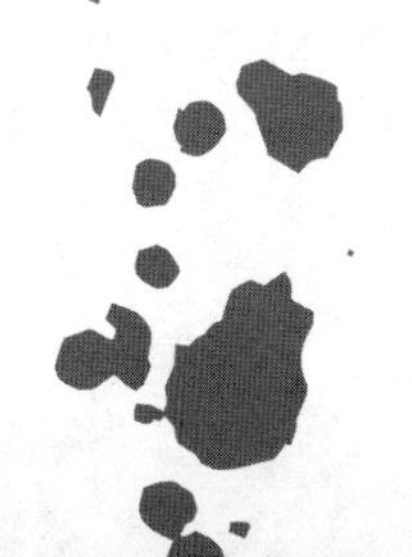

Now for the tricky bit if you find yourself asking the way in New Zealand. Here goes... 'Taumatawhakatangihangak oauauotamateaturipukaka pikimaungahoronukupokaiwhe nua kitanatahu' (85 letters)

This is a hill in New Zealand – it is a Maori phrase which means 'the place where Tamatea, the man with the big knees, who slid, climbed and swallowed mountains, known as land-eater, played his flute to his loved one'.

The *Guinness Book of Records* still regards this as the longest place name on earth but there is a longer name for Bangkok in Thailand. Take a deep breath for this mouthful:
'Krung thep maha nakorn amorn ratana kosinmahintar ayutthay amaha dilok phop noppa ratrajathani burirom udom rajaniwesmahasat harn amorn phimarn avatarn sathit sakkattiya visanukamprasit'.

Guess what it means... 'The City – eternal treasure, the impregnable city of God Indra, the grand capital of the world endowed with nine precious stones, the happy city, where resides the Royal Palace that resembles the heavenly abode where reigns the reincarnated god, a city given by Indra and built by Vishnukarnom'. Phew!

The third longest geographical name in the world can be found in Wales. It is the longest village name in the world and many people go there just to take a selfie by the sign.

anfairpwllgwyngyllgogerychwyrndrobwllllantysiliogogogoch in Anglesey means 'Saint Mary's Church in the hollow of the white hazel near a rapid whirlpool and the Church of St. Tysilio of the red cave'. The OGO at the end comes from the word 'ogof' meaning 'cave' in Welsh. You can now put your teeth back in.

10 random Earth-shattering facts (spot the foulest!)

1 Continents shift on 'plates' at about the same rate as your fingernails grow. The greatest movement occurs at the Tonga microplate, near Samoa, which is moving steadily further into the Pacific at a rate of 24 centimetres (9.4 inches) per year.

2 Mount Thor on Baffin Island, Canada, has Earth's greatest sheer vertical drop of 1,250 metres (4,100 feet). You can take one step off the peak and fall nearly a mile before you hit anything. It's probably best not to try this without a parachute.

3 In the Philippines, there's an island that's within a lake, on an island that's within a lake, on an island. You might need to read that again! It's Lake Taal on Luzon Island, with a volcano in the middle of it and a crater lake within that.

4 While elephants and whales are considered the largest living creatures in the world, the title of the largest known living thing on the planet goes to the Great Barrier Reef off the Australian coast.

Stretching to about 2,000 kilometres (1,243 miles) and covering an area of around 217,480 square kilometres (135,136 square miles), this 'living body' is made up of 3,000 individual reefs and 900 coral islands. Known as the largest living structure on Earth, it is visible from space.

The world's greatest land mountain range is the Himalayas, stretching 2,253 kilometres (1,400 miles) and containing 96 of the world's 109 peaks that are over 7,315 metres (24,000 feet) high. And guess what… this mountain range continues to rise more than 1 centimetre per year.

6 A far bigger mountain range is under the sea. Spanning nearly 65,000 kilometres (40,389 miles), the mid-ocean ridge is the world's longest mountain range. As the name suggests, almost 90% of it lies deep down under the oceans and it consists of many active volcanoes.

7 The deepest point on Earth is in the ocean at the Mariana Trench in the Pacific Ocean, which is where the five deepest trenches in the world are found, with a depth of more than 10,668 metres (35,000 feet) and stretching for 2,542 kilometres (1,580 miles) – more than five times the length of the Grand Canyon. The deepest part of the trench is 2,147 metres (7,043 feet) deeper than Everest is tall – that's getting on for 11 kilometres (7 miles) deep. The bottom of the Mariana Trench is covered with a blanket of icky, gungy ooze as, owing to the immense water pressure, everything gets squashed to a pulp and ends up as a fine, silky sludge. If you thought of going down there, you'd also become instant cheesy splodge.

8 Yellowstone National Park in the USA is actually a huge volcano. Its most recent eruption was before humans lived. It hurled ash all the way to the Gulf of Mexico. It is dormant, which means it could blow up at any time, although a massive eruption is not expected for another 1,000 to 10,000 years. Fingers crossed!

90% of Earth's human population lives in the Northern Hemisphere.

Foul alert...

There are about 7 billion people on Earth and together we produce over 1 million tons of poop a day. That's getting on for 115 Eiffel Towers made of excrement. It would take about 417 Olympic-sized swimming pools to hold all the human poop we produce in a single day. Best not go for a dip in one of them!

Knock knock time

Knock, knock, who's there?
Kenya.
Kenya who?
Kenya think of anything that's more fun than geography?

Knock, knock, who's there?
Waterfall.
Waterfall who?
Waterfall I am not to like geography.

Knock, knock, who's there?
Ammonia.
Ammonia who?
Ammonia beginner but I love geography already.

The joy of geography

My dad grounded me for getting a terrible Geography result at school. So I said, 'How am I meant to do better and learn more about the world if I'm not allowed to leave my room?' He said, 'Try Google Earth.' So I googled 'Earth' and found it's the third planet from the Sun and the only object in the universe known to have intelligent life. A shame it's not found in geography class.

My dad said Google Earth gave him the opportunity to visit anywhere in the world. So what did he do? He just looked at our house!

A hardened geographer

A geography student named Harris
Whom nothing could ever embarrass
Took a bath in tutorial,
Which became his memorial...
As the bath salts were plaster of Paris.

Did you hear on the news that Yorkshire Police had all their maps stolen by a serial geography fanatic? A spokesman said they are still searching for Leeds.

I love maps. I'd feel lost without them.

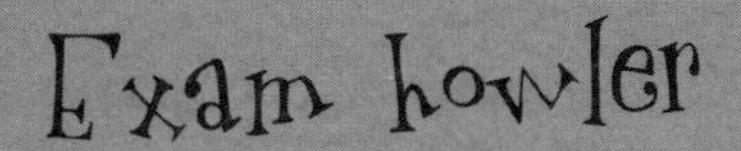

In a geography exam, a question asked: name one measure that can be put in place to avoid flooding in times of heavy rainfall. One answer said: 'Flooding in areas such as the Mississippi can be avoided by placing a number of big dames in the river'. Now that would cause a splash!

Silly joke

Two geographers are hiking in the woods when one is bitten on the bottom by a snake. The other says, 'I'll go into town for a doctor.'
Using all his map skills, he runs ten miles to a small town and finds the only doctor delivering a baby.
'I can't leave,' the doctor says. 'But here's what to do. Take a knife, cut a little X where the bite is, suck out the poison and spit it on the ground.'
The geographer runs back to his friend, who is in agony and crying, 'What did the doctor say?'
'He says there's no way you'll get the poison out. I'm afraid you're going to die.'

Habitats

Geographers study all kinds of habitats. In case you forgot, a habitat is an environment in which particular plants and animals live.

Tropical rainforest

This habitat is AMAZING. Rainforests used to cover 14% of the Earth's surface, but due to deforestation (people chopping them down), they now only cover around 6%. About half of all animal and plant species on earth live there. WOW facts:

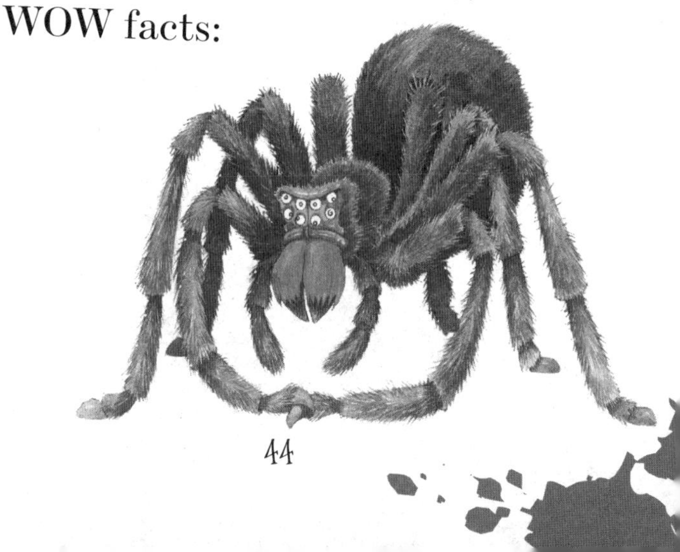

Rainforests get at least 250 centimetres (98 inches) of rain a year. Sometimes it's almost double that at 450 centimetres (177 inches). That's wet – and steamy.

It can take ten minutes for a falling raindrop to travel from a rainforest's thick leaf canopy to the floor.

A quarter of ingredients in modern medicines come from rainforest plants.

Scientists believe that there may be millions of plant and insect species in rainforests that have yet to be discovered.

80% of the flowers in Australian rainforests are not found anywhere else in the world.

The Amazon rainforest in South America is the world's largest tropical rainforest. Covering over 2 million square miles, it's so big that the UK and Ireland would fit into it 17 times!

6 Amazon fast facts

1 The Amazon River and its forests stretch across Peru, Bolivia, Venezuela, Colombia, Ecuador and Brazil.

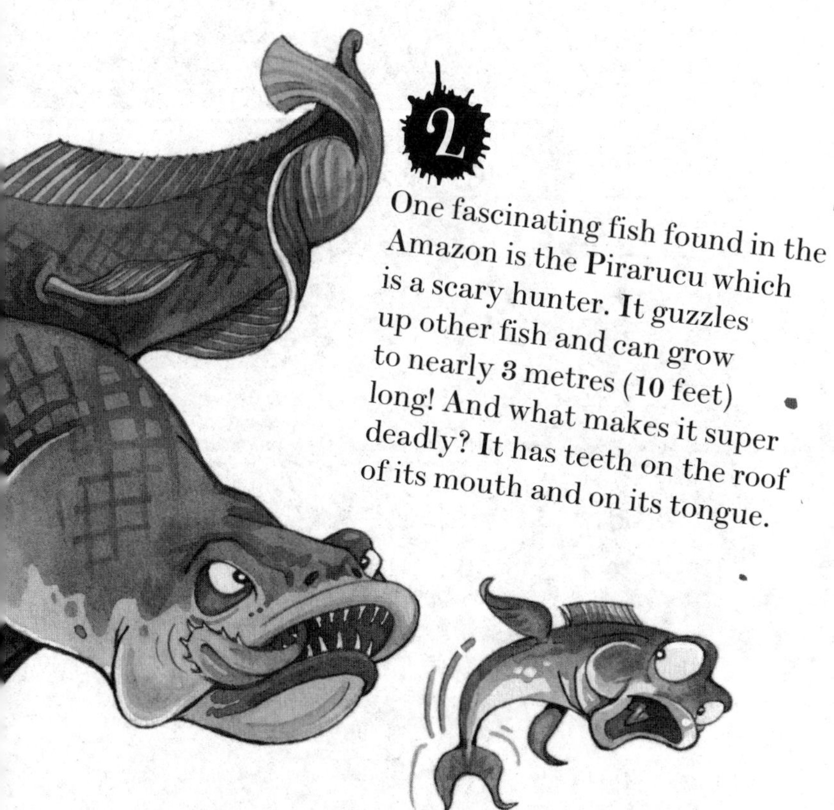

2

One fascinating fish found in the Amazon is the Pirarucu which is a scary hunter. It guzzles up other fish and can grow to nearly 3 metres (10 feet) long! And what makes it super deadly? It has teeth on the roof of its mouth and on its tongue.

3

The Amazon has an incredibly rich habitat – there are around 40,000 plant species, 1,300 bird species, 3,000 types of fish, 430 mammals and a whopping 2.5 million different insects. Wow!

4 The Amazon is home to a whole host of fascinating (and deadly) creatures, including electric eels, flesh-eating piranha fish, poison dart frogs, jaguars and some seriously venomous snakes.

5 Around 400–500 tribes call the Amazon rainforest home. It's believed that about fifty of these tribes have never had contact with the outside world.

6 Rainforests are often called 'the lungs of the Earth' because the rich vegetation takes carbon dioxide out of the air and releases oxygen back in. More than 20% of the world's oxygen is produced by the Amazon rainforest.

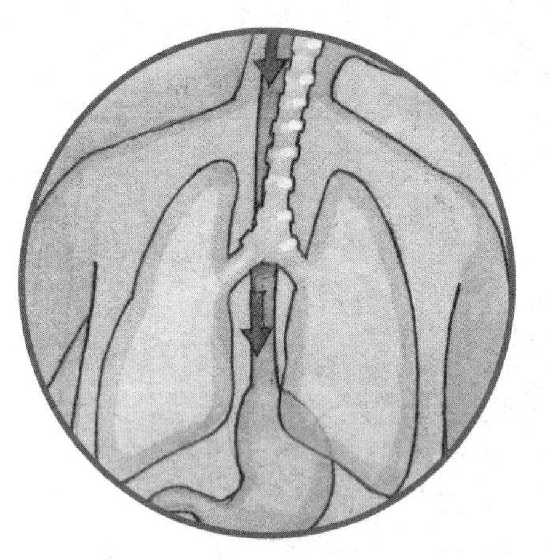

A geographer entered the jungle
But made an incredible bungle
By setting up camp
In the mouldiest damp...
His pants fell apart, foul and fungal.

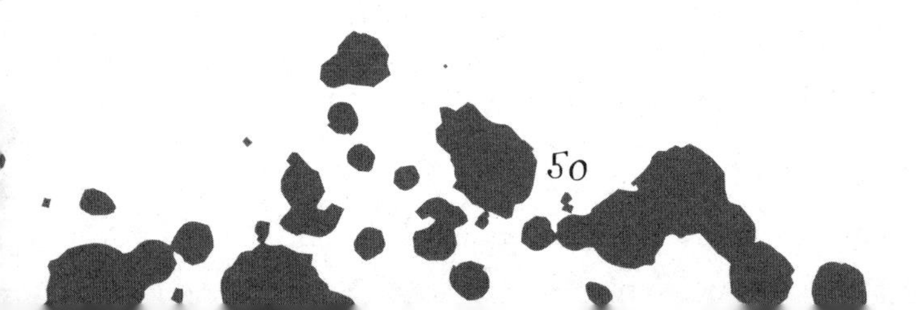

STINK ALERT

Due to the thickness of the canopy (the top branches and leaves of the trees), much of the floor in rainforests is in permanent darkness. It can also be hot, smelly, steamy and mouldy. Things rot (decompose) about 10 times quicker in tropical rainforests than in other habitats. If you hang around too long on that damp forest floor, you'd start to pong, too.

Stinkhorn is a type of fungus that thrives in tropical rainforests. It smells like rotting food and dung, to attract flies. You wouldn't want spores of that fungi to find their way into your pants!

Daft jungly joke

A geographer and a zoologist wearing bobble hats are hiking through the rainforest when a monkey drops from a branch, grabs the geographer's hat and darts off with it. The geographer is furious when the monkey starts nibbling the woolly hat, while the zoologist is fascinated by such behaviour.
'The monkey must like you,' the zoologist smiled. 'I expect it's a fan of geography!'
'Well, I don't like it, and I don't like your attitude,' the geographer snapped.
The zoologist replied with a wink, 'It's not MY attitude, it's your hat-he-chewed!'

Geography
is monkeying around
in habitats in shabby-hats!

Deserts

Some of the driest areas of our planet receive less than 40cm (15.7 inches) of rain a year. That's not much to keep many plants and animals alive. In fact, hot deserts such as the Sahara in Africa can have no rain at all in some years. A town named Tidikelt in the Sahara desert did not receive a drop of rain for ten years.

Did you know?

Not all deserts are hot and only about 20% of the deserts on Earth are covered in sand. Many of the ice-free regions of the Arctic and Antarctic are known as polar deserts. That's because they lose more moisture than they gain. Together with the severe cold, these are some of the harshest habitats on our planet. One of the driest places on Earth is in the valleys of the Antarctic near Ross Island. There has been no rainfall there for two million years. However, in parts of the Atacama Desert in Chile, no rain has ever been recorded. Scientists believe such areas have been in an extreme desert state for 40 million years – longer than any other place on Earth.

Scary stuff

Did you know that deserts don't always form naturally? Some are man-made by accident because of the way humans treat the land. We allow animals to over-graze and let their hooves damage the soil. Then soil and plants start disappearing. Once the vegetation is stripped, the soil gets blown away and nothing will grow. This is called desertification.
Some deserts are growing because of human activity and global warming. The Sahara desert is expanding at a rate of about 48 kilometres (30 miles) south per year.

After those nasty facts, it's time to lighten the mood with desert jokes:

Three geographers are in a desert. The first says, 'I brought some water so we don't die of thirst.'
The second says, 'I brought some suntan lotion so we don't get sunburned.'
Then the third says 'I brought a car door.'
The others ask, 'Why did you bring that?'
'Ah,' came the reply, 'so I can roll down the window and we'll all keep cool.'

A geographer is lost in the Sahara Desert. He used up the last of his water three days ago and he lies gasping on the sand, when in the distance he hears barking. Propping himself up on one elbow, he squints against the sun and sees an Eskimo bundled up in furs, driving a sled with a team of huskies across the dunes. Thinking that he's going mad, the geographer blinks and shakes his head, but it's for real. He feebly calls, 'Help!' The Eskimo steers the sled towards him, the huskies panting in the heat. The geographer croaks, 'Am I pleased to see you! I've been wandering around this desert for days, my water's all gone and I'm completely lost.' The perspiring Eskimo looks down at him and sighs, '**YOU'RE** lost?!'

Silly story

A geography professor is dying of thirst in the desert. At last he sees an oasis ahead and staggers to it. When he gets there, it turns out that it was just a couple of trees. No water. Just a mirage.

He continues searching, and sees some men up ahead of him. He notices they look like salesmen, as they're wearing suits and holding briefcases.

'Hey!' the professor calls, waving to get the salesmen's attention. He runs over to them. 'Do you...have any...water?' he pants.

'Sorry, sir,' the first salesman answers, 'we only sell ties.'
'Ties? Don't you have some water?'
'No, sir.'
The professor brushes past them, grumbling that ties are totally useless. Still desperate for water, he plods on and sees a pool in front of him. Hundreds of people are swimming, as fountains spray high into the sky. It's not a mirage this time. Two men are standing at the gate. The professor staggers towards them.
'Excuse me,' he croaks, 'will you let me in? I'm dying of thirst and I need water. I just need one drink!'
'Sorry sir,' the security guard says, 'but we only allow in people wearing ties.'

Even sillier

Three geographers were walking through the desert under a baking sun. They were fully equipped with enough water and food for days. On the shimmering horizon they saw mirages of swimming pools, stalls full of ice-cream and ice-cool drinks. But the geographers did not crack, they kept plodding on to study the area and draw their maps.

Suddenly one of them froze. 'Psssst,' he pointed. His companions halted, and strained their eyes to where he was pointing. 'Look – isn't that a bacon tree on the horizon?'

And sure enough, there it stood in the middle of the desert – an oasis with a bacon tree and the wafting smell of burgers. Slowly they crept forwards until they were within a stone's throw of the bacon tree. Suddenly, a shot rang out, knocking one of the geographers down in his tracks. As the others bandaged him and poured water over his face, they could hear his faint voice. 'That was no bacon tree,' he gasped, 'that was a ham bush.'

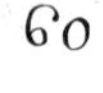

Mountains

Mountain habitats can be awesome, scary, exciting and dangerous all at once. That might be because they attract hoards of geographers in woolly hats and rucksacks who will all delight in telling you at least 10 useful facts about these tall lumps of rock sticking up into the sky.

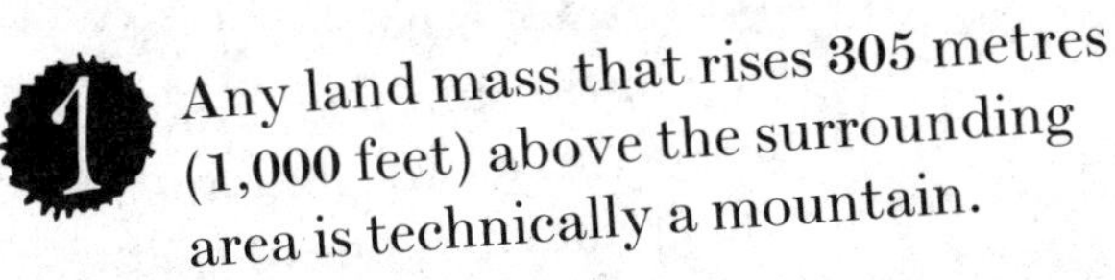

1 Any land mass that rises 305 metres (1,000 feet) above the surrounding area is technically a mountain.

2 Scottish mountains over 305 metres (1,000 feet) are called Munros. British mountains and hills over 150 metres (492 feet) high are sometimes called Marilyns.

3 More than half of the world's fresh water comes from mountains and all the major rivers in the world are fed from mountain sources. Wow!

4 Fold mountains are the most common type of mountain. The world's largest mountain ranges are fold mountains (the Himalayas, the Rockies, the Alps). These ranges were formed over millions of years when two plates pushed together head on, and their edges crumbled, much the same way as a piece of paper folds when pushed. Some of these mountains are still growing.

Over 6,000 people have now climbed Mount Everest, including a 13-year-old American in 2010. The first wedding at the summit was in 2005.

6 In 1974, a German team that had set out to climb Mount Annapurna 4 was reported to have reached the top of Annapurna 2 by mistake. Oops – always read the map!

7 Some mountains are caused by volcanoes spewing lava over hundreds of years. The lava cools and hardens and builds up to form a mountain. The islands of Hawaii are actually volcanoes. Sometimes lava doesn't erupt through the crust, but builds up under the surface to push up a mountain. This is called a dome mountain.

8 Fault block mountains occur when the tectonic plates collide with each other and form cracks in the earth's surface. Rocks are pushed upward when this happens.

Plateau mountains look like tall squares with flat tops. Plateaus form when the earth's plates collide with each other, but don't buckle the surface.

In 1950, a four-month-old kitten
climbed 4,478 metres (14,691 feet) to
the top of the Matterhorn in the Alps.
Maybe it was bored and wanted summit
to do – and achieved the world record by
a whisker.

*Kathmandu is in the Himalayas.

'I can't understand why men make all this fuss about Everest – it's only a mountain.'

Junko Tabei – first woman to climb Everest (in 1975).

Cheesy one-liners

What's the best cheese to coax a bear down a mountain? Camembert (come on bear?!)

Mountains aren't just funny, they're hill areas (hilarious)!

How do mountains see? They peak.

Plateau: the highest form of flattery.

Did you hear about the geography student who went up a mountain scree slope to conquer his fear of avalanches? He wanted to get a little boulder.

Silly story

When my doctor asked me about what I did yesterday, I told him about my day.
'Well, yesterday afternoon, I waded across the edge of a lake, escaped from a mountain lion in the heavy brush, hiked up and down a mountain, hacked my way through rainforest, crawled out of quicksand and plodded through miles of desert.'
The doctor said: 'You must be an awesome geographer.'
'No,' I replied, 'I'm just a terrible golfer.'

Loopy limerick

A geographer studying rocks
Chipped away at a cliff-edge of blocks.
If only they'd told her
Of the unstable boulder...
They carried her home in a box.

Just in case you were wondering… the fear of mountains is called Orophobia (from the ancient Greek *oros* meaning 'mountain'). The fear of volcanoes (understandable) is called Volcanophobia.

Volcanoes

At least 1,500 active volcanoes are often puffing away around the world, and some of them have been erupting for years. They form when molten rock called magma breaks through a weak area of Earth's surface. The chambers that contain magma can quietly lurk underground for hundreds of years, and then erupt with surprising force.

Did you know...

The volcanic rock pumice is the only rock that can float in water. It is usually grey and full of bubbly holes, which form when hot gases pop out of the rock as it cools.

The most powerful volcanoes are called supervolcanoes, which can pour smoke and ash over thousands of miles, causing worldwide climate change. These monsters only stir every few hundred thousand years. So, keep sleeping, Yellowstone! The largest eruption ever observed was of Mount Tambora on the island of Sumbawa, in Indonesia. Its eruption in 1815 killed about 100,000 people. Indonesia has over 70 active volcanoes today.

The biggest volcano on Earth is Hawaii's Mauna Loa. It is one of five volcanoes in Hawaii and towers nearly 4,000 metres (13,123 feet) above sea level.

Most volcanoes occur near the edges of tectonic plates, the massive rock slabs that make up Earth's surface. But some volcanoes, such as the Yellowstone supervolcano, lie over other 'hot spots' where magma wells up from deep within the Earth. One day it will burst out and kaboom!

Scared of being toasted by a volcano? Well, don't panic TOO much. There are about 7 billion people on earth, with about 500 million living in volcanic zones. Every year an average of 1,000 deaths are caused by volcanic activity.

So, if you approach an active volcano and ignore safety warnings then your risk increases (surprise, surprise!). But volcanoes are less dangerous than other hazards in life. Someone has kept awake at night worrying and working these out:

	Chance of dying
playing sport	1 in 5,000
taking bath	1 in 10,000
storm	1 in 17,000
bee sting	1 in 76,000
volcanic eruption	1 in 80,000

So sleep tight (unless you take a bath on a volcano with a bee in a storm).

Areas with volcanoes often have earthquakes because fault lines in the earth's crust can develop in such 'hot spots'. Here are some earth-shattering reminders:

The area around Japan in the Pacific Ocean has the most earthquakes in the world. This area also has a lot of volcanoes. It is called the Ring of Fire.

Underneath the Earth's surface lie tectonic plates which shift over time. Sometimes they slide under one another or push up against each other, creating enormous stress. When they move again, they judder and cause an earthquake.

Around half a million earthquakes shake parts of the world every year. Only a small amount can be felt and fewer than a hundred cause serious damage.

The deadliest earthquake on record took place in China in 1556 when about 830,000 people died as their homes collapsed.

Scientists who study earthquakes are called seismologists. They can tell how serious an earthquake is by a machine called a seismogram, which measures the intensity of the quakes. An earthquake rated 3 to 5 is minor, an earthquake rated 5 to 7 is moderate to strong, an earthquake rated 7 to 8 is major and an earthquake rated 8 or above is great. Seismophobia is the fear of all earthquakes – and probably very common in some parts of the world!

On average, one earthquake measuring 8 or above happens every year.

Earthquakes can trigger a tsunami, which is a huge wave of water in oceans or lakes. Volcanic eruptions and landslides can also set off a massive tsunami.

What did the tectonic plate say to the other tectonic plate when they bumped into each other?
'Sorry, my fault.'

Random rivers

In 2007, a man named Martin Strel swam the entire length of the Amazon River. His jungle journey took ten hours a day for 66 days. He probably swam much faster where there were piranha fish! If he swims the Nile next, he'll probably go into denial (de Nile).

Running through the north of the Amazon rainforest is the Amazon river. It flows for almost 6,437 kilometres (4,000 miles) and is the second longest river in the world. The longest is the river Nile, stretching over 6,598 kilometres (4,100 miles).

The longest river in the USA is the Missouri River. It is 3,765 kilometres (2,340 miles) long (slightly longer than the Mississippi River).

Most of the world's major cities are found on or near the banks of rivers.

The Ganges, Yangtze and Indus rivers are three of the most polluted on Earth. **FOUL ALERT**: If you fall in and swallow the water, you might never come out alive. Chemicals, human poo and the occasional dead body could be swirling around you!

River puns

Have you read the book *One Big River* by my teacher, Mrs. Sippy?

I like the scenery around river valleys. Some can be absolutely gorges.

Q: What has five eyes and is lying on the water?
A: The Mississippi river.

Geography test

Teacher: Name three different animals that give milk.
Pupil: A goat, a cow and Mr Jenkins who works at the supermarket dairy counter.
Teacher: On which side of the globe is Central America?
Pupil: The outside.
Teacher: What's the difference between an African elephant and an Indian elephant?
Pupil: Their postcodes.
Teacher: What do you know about Iceland?
Pupil: It's only a 'c' away from Ireland.
Teacher: Doh!

Awesome oceans

As the 'blue planet', the Earth is influenced by the huge oceans. Did you know:

1. Most of the world's oxygen (about 70%) comes from seaweeds and other microscopic algae in the oceans.

2. There could be nine times more microscopic algae and seaweeds in the oceans than there are plants on land.

3. Seaweeds are amongst the fastest growing organisms on the planet. The giant kelp can grow nearly 1 metre (3 feet) a day – reaching lengths of over 50 metres (164 feet).

Down under

Australia is the biggest island on Earth, although some geographers call it a 'continental land mass totally surrounded by ocean'. Yes, even though Australia is surrounded by water, it doesn't have the world's longest coastline at 25,749 kilometres (16,000 miles). In fact, Australia ranks seventh on the list of the world's longest coastlines, coming in behind Canada with a whopping 244,781 kilometres (152,100 miles) of coast. But, just for the record, Australia is wider than the Moon.

Mystery time

The Bermuda Triangle is a particular area of the Atlantic Ocean between Florida, Puerto Rico and Bermuda. This 'triangle' covers about 804,762 square kilometres (500,000 square miles) and is where many ships and planes have disappeared over the years. It is also an area where magnetic compasses seem to operate differently from normal.

So what causes this? Aliens? Sea monsters? Unknown forces? Or have reports about the Bermuda Triangle been exaggerated? Try these well-known stories:

1 In 1918 a Navy cargo ship called the USS Cyclops sank in the Bermuda Triangle. The Cyclops had equipment to send out an SOS distress call to signal to other ships that it needed help, but the ship never sent out the message. No one ever found out what happened and why it vanished so quickly.

2 In 1941 two ships with the same design as the USS Cyclops also mysteriously disappeared very close to the same location. That's weird, don't you think?

3 In 1945, five Navy bomber planes with fourteen passengers flew from Fort Lauderdale, Florida on a practice bombing mission known as Flight 19. When compasses stopped working on board, all five planes got lost. The planes flew on until they ran out of fuel. A rescue plane disappeared on the same day. The Navy searched for the wreckage and crew of Flight 19 for weeks, but the planes and crew had disappeared without a trace. Spooky.

Scientists say the number of disappearances in the Bermuda Triangle is not abnormal, even though some of these disappearances have been very strange. Despite the area's scary reputation, disasters are apparently not that common there. Boats and planes travel safely through the Bermuda Triangle every day. So maybe it's just a fuss over nothing. What do you think? Don't have nightmares!

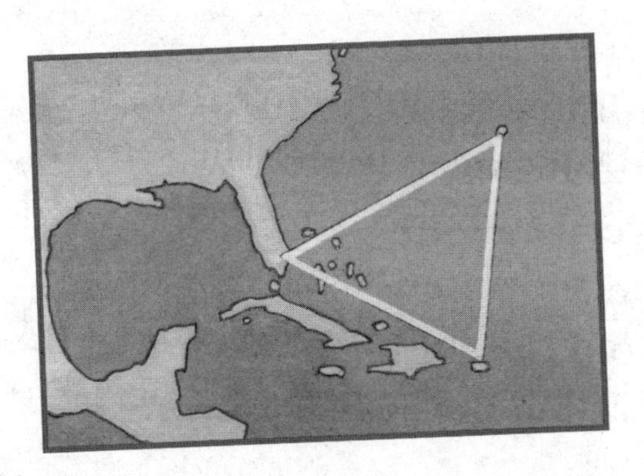

CheeSEA nonsense

What is purple, has a lot of coral and lies in the ocean near Australia?
The Grape Barrier Reef.

Last night I dreamed the whole ocean was full of orange fizz. Apparently, it was just a Fanta sea.

Then I had a nightmare that I was diving deep under the sea. It got very embarrassing at the sight of the enormous ocean's wobbly bottom – all bumpy, bubbling and covered in barnacles.

World population

Geographers are fascinated about where people choose to live. Long ago most people lived in small rural communities, but today more of us prefer to live in towns or cities. This is called urbanisation. If you're a geographer, you'll tingle with excitement and ask 'why?'

Cue for a limerick...

A geographer went on vacation,
Missed her train and got stuck
at the station.
'Oh dear, what a pity,
I'll camp here in the city
And contribute to urbanisation.'

City facts

to impress your friends (or bore them senseless)

1 The largest city by population in the world is Shanghai in China. With about 24 million people, the city's population will be controlled to keep it at around 25 million by 2035.

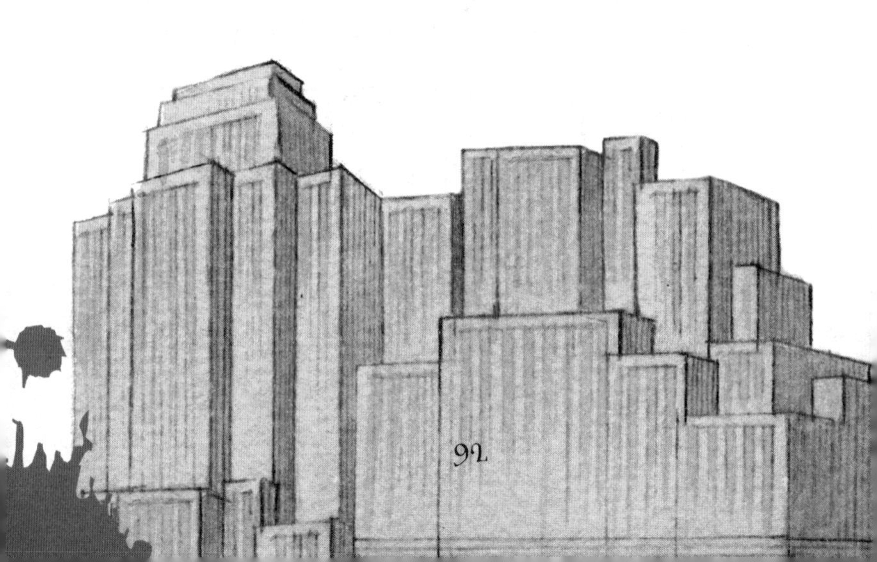

2 The highest city in the world is the Peruvian town of La Rinconada, which is at a breathless 5,100 metres (16,732 feet) above sea level.

3 The stinkiest city is said to be Rotorua in New Zealand, because of all the natural geysers. Nicknamed 'Sulphur City', Rotorua was built on top of a volcanic hot spot, with the steamy whiff of rotten eggs wafting through the streets.

5 trivial city facts to remember before bed:

Amsterdam (in the Netherlands) has more bikes than people. There are approximately 1 million of them (bikes, that is).

Barcelona (Spain) is one of the worst places to drive in the world, with an accident happening on average every 19 seconds (maybe it's the same bad driver each time).

3 Berlin (Germany) was the first place in Europe to have traffic lights (yawn!).

New York's Central Park is one of the world's largest urban parks (zzzz).

Istanbul (Turkey) is the only city in 2 continents – it is in Asia and Europe (snore).

Fascinating figures

to make geographers leap out of bed with excitement:

Despite urbanisation, all cities in the world take up only about 1% of the Earth's land area.

In 1800, only 2% of the world's population lived in towns or cities. By 2030, about 60% of all people will live in urban areas.

In 2000, the world population reached 6.1 billion, and is growing at an annual rate of 1.2% (77 million people per year).

By 2030, probably 85% of the world's population will be in developing countries.

By 2050, the number of people older than 60 years will more than triple to about 2 billion. The number of people over 80 years of age will increase even more, to 379 million in 2050, more than a five-fold increase. In other words, the world will be full of grey hair!

Knock, knock!
Who's there?
Havana.
Havana who?
Havana a wonderful time here in the capital city of Cuba!

Q: What city always cheats at exams?
A: Peking (even though it's now called Beijing, so the joke doesn't work!)

Wacky weather

Weather and climate are all part of geography – or, if you want the proper term for it: meteorology. That must be worth a few cheesy jokes…

What's the difference between weather and climate?
You can't weather a tree, but you can climate!
(Actually, weather is the condition of the atmosphere over a short period, while climate is the average atmospheric conditions over a longer period.)

There's a technical term for
a sunny, warm day which
follows two rainy days.
It's called Monday.

Where did the meteorologist
stop for a drink on the way
home from a long day in the
weather forecast studio?
The nearest **ISOBAR**.
Tee hee.

Foul alert

Did you know that rain isn't always made of water drops? Brace yourself...

In 1932 in Elgin, Canada, it rained sizzling geese. 52 geese flying overhead were struck by lightning, singed to a frazzle and fell in the streets ready-cooked!

In 1968 in Mexico during a boat race, the crowd got covered in maggots. Yes, the clouds rained down live, wriggly maggots!

In many counties, including the UK, it has often rained fish and frogs splatting down from the sky. That's because a column of wind called a waterspout can suck up water from a pond, carry it overland, then drop everything as rain – slimy, smelly pondweed included. Yuck!

If it ever rains cats and dogs, be careful you don't step in a poodle!

Climate Change

Earth's weather and climates have always been changing over millions of years for all sorts of reasons. Today, many scientists are worried that human activity is warming up the planet, which could melt the polar ice, causing huge floods and many other environmental disasters.

The Earth warmed by an average of 1°C in the last century, and although that doesn't seem much, it means big things for people and wildlife around the globe. Rising temperatures don't mean we'll all get nicer weather – but we're likely to get more extreme weather.

Growing amounts of carbon dioxide cause a 'greenhouse effect' by warming up the Earth's surface. Some of that carbon dioxide comes from plants and volcanoes, but people are now responsible for most of it. According to the U.S. Geological Survey (USGS), the world's volcanoes throw out about 200 million tons of carbon dioxide a year (1% of the total), while cars and factories pump out 24 billion tons of carbon dioxide every year worldwide.

5 scary facts scientists tell us:

1. Every single day, 70 million tons of carbon dioxide are released into our world's atmosphere.

2. Ships can now sail along the Northwest Passage, as melting Arctic ice from global warming has opened this route for the first time in over 100 years.

3 Arctic summers could be ice-free by 2040. The effects of global warming will increase as the oceans absorb more of the sun's heat. This melting ice will cause polar bears and other species to lose their habitat and eventually become extinct.

82% of glaciers have disappeared in Glacier National Park, Montana. Today this beautiful park has only 27 glaciers, compared with 150 in 1910.

Over a hundred million people will be displaced by just a 1 metre (3 foot) rise in sea levels. Many scientists predict that the oceans will rise at least this much by 2100.

Geography teacher: How do you intend to reduce your carbon footprints in the future?

Pupil: Take bigger steps.

Geography teacher: I mean how are you going to save energy?

Pupil: Easy – stay in bed.

Geography teacher: If we produce 48% more carbon emissions than we did in the 1970s, how can that figure be halved?

Pupil: Just divide it by two.

Geography teacher: But don't you realise, since you've been sitting there 2,000 hectares of rainforest have been destroyed.

Pupil: In that case, shall I sit at the back?

Geography teacher: What do you think about greenhouse gases and CFCs?

Pupil: Ooh, I love chocolate fudge cake in the conservatory.

Geography teacher: Doh!

Global warming
(daft story)

Because of climate change, a great forest fire raged out of control. A geography professor wanted to get close-up photos of the fire. Smoke at the scene was too thick to get good shots, so the professor hired a plane.

'It will be waiting for you at the airport,' the pilot said on the phone.

Sure enough, a plane was waiting near the runway. The professor jumped in and yelled, 'Let's go! Let's go!'

The pilot swung the plane into the wind and soon they were high in the air.

'Fly over the north side of the fire,' said the professor, 'and make three or four low-level passes.'
'Why?' asked the pilot.
'Because I'm going to take pictures and analyse data. I'm a professor, and professors study evidence, use their powers of observation and make informed decisions. That's what I'm paid for. I'm famous for my wise judgements.'
After a long pause the pilot stuttered, 'So you mean you're not the flying instructor?'

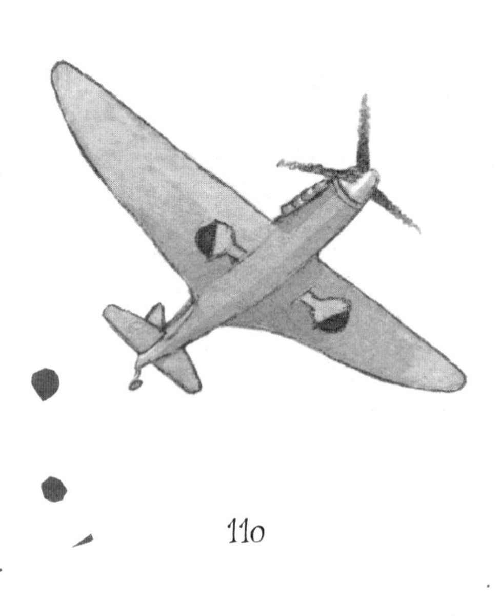

The geography of poo

No book in this series is complete without a peep at some poop.
In fact, global sanitation is a serious subject, as health and hygiene around the world are still a major problem. Here are some of the foul facts from the World Health Organisation (WHO) and the United Nations Children's Fund (UNICEF):

1 Around 60% of the world's population – 4.5 billion people – don't have access to a proper toilet.

2 862 million people around the world have to squat on the ground for their toilet.

3 1.8 billion people use drinking water with likely contamination from excrement.

Globally, 80% of waste water and sewage flows into rivers without being treated.

With safe water and good hygiene, improved sanitation could prevent around 842,000 deaths each year.

Dirty nappies are only the tip of a mountain of human excrement produced around the globe every day. The challenge will be how to deal with the growing output of poo as the world's population creeps towards 10 billion by 2100.

And finally...

If you said you were from South America, I wouldn't Bolivia.

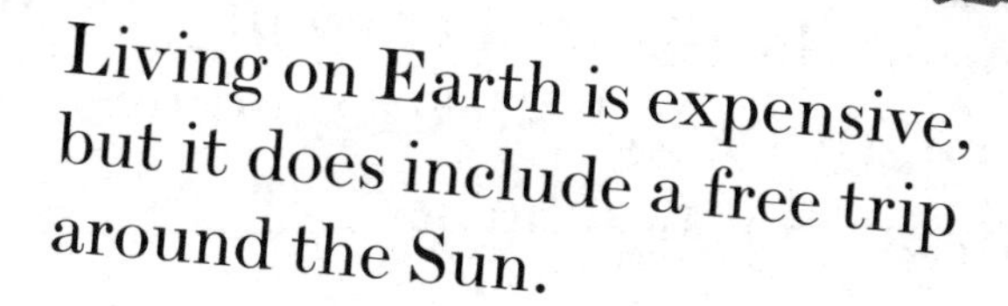

Living on Earth is expensive, but it does include a free trip around the Sun.

I saw a geography documentary on transport and how ships are kept together.
It was riveting.

I saw a geography documentary on farming where a farmer counted 196 cows in the field before rounding them up. So then he had 200.

Have you noticed that bottled water has a 'best before' date printed on it?
That water has circled the earth for 4 billion years... but on that date it's ruined!

I can't spell Armageddon. But then again, it's not the end of the world.

If you survived some of the truly foul facts and cheesy jokes in this book, take a look at the other wacky titles in this revolting series. They're all guaranteed to make you groan and squirm like never before. Share them with your friends **AT YOUR OWN RISK!**

QUIZ

1. What makes up over 68% of the Earth's surface?

a) Mud

b) Ice

c) Salt water

2. What is the difference between the hottest and coldest temperatures recorded on Earth?

a) Over 150°C

b) Almost 1000 °C

c) Just under 100°C

3. What is the largest known living thing on our planet?

a) A blue whale

b) The Great Barrier Reef

c) Seaweed

4. Where do most people live on Earth?

a) China

b) The northern hemisphere

c) New York

5. Where is the world's largest tropical rainforest?

a) The African Bowl

b) The Australian Sink

c) The Amazon Basin

6. When magma (molten rock) erupts from a volcano, what is it called?

a) Lather

b) Lava

c) Palaver

7. Which area is on top of a supervolcano that could explode one day?

a) Yellowstone Park

b) Blueridge Mountains

c) Redrock Desert

8. Which of these is true?

a) In 2000, the world population reached 6.1 billion

b) Cities in the world now take up 10% of the Earth's land area

c) By 2050 85% of the world's population will have grey hair

9. What is the Bermuda Triangle?

a) Three islands in the Bahamas

b) An area in the North Atlantic Ocean

c) Fabric used to make Bermuda shorts

10. Which of these is false?

a) Over 80% of glaciers have disappeared in Glacier National Park, Montana

b) 80% of the world's population don't use toilets

c) 80% of the world's sewage flows into rivers without being treated

Answers:

1= c
2= a
3= b
4= b
5= c
6= b
7= a
8= a
9= b
10= b

GLOSSARY

Asteroid: one of the many large rocks in space that orbit the sun.

Equator: an imaginary line circling the middle of the earth.

Glacier: a large body of ice moving very slowly down a slope or valley.

Greenhouse gas: gases in the atmosphere (e.g. water vapour, carbon dioxide and methane) that trap heat energy from the sun that would otherwise escape back into space.

Lava: hot liquid rock from under the earth which pours from volcanoes before cooling and hardening.

Meteor: material from outer space that enters the earth's atmosphere and burns up in a streak of light.

Meteoroid: space debris that can be from a few millimetres to a kilometre in size.

Reef: a hard ridge stretching under the surface of the sea, made of rock or coral (formed from small sea creatures).

INDEX

I finished reading this Truly Foul & Cheesy book on:

........../........../..........